THE COMIC ADVENTURES
OF OLD MOTHER HUBBARD
AND HER DOG

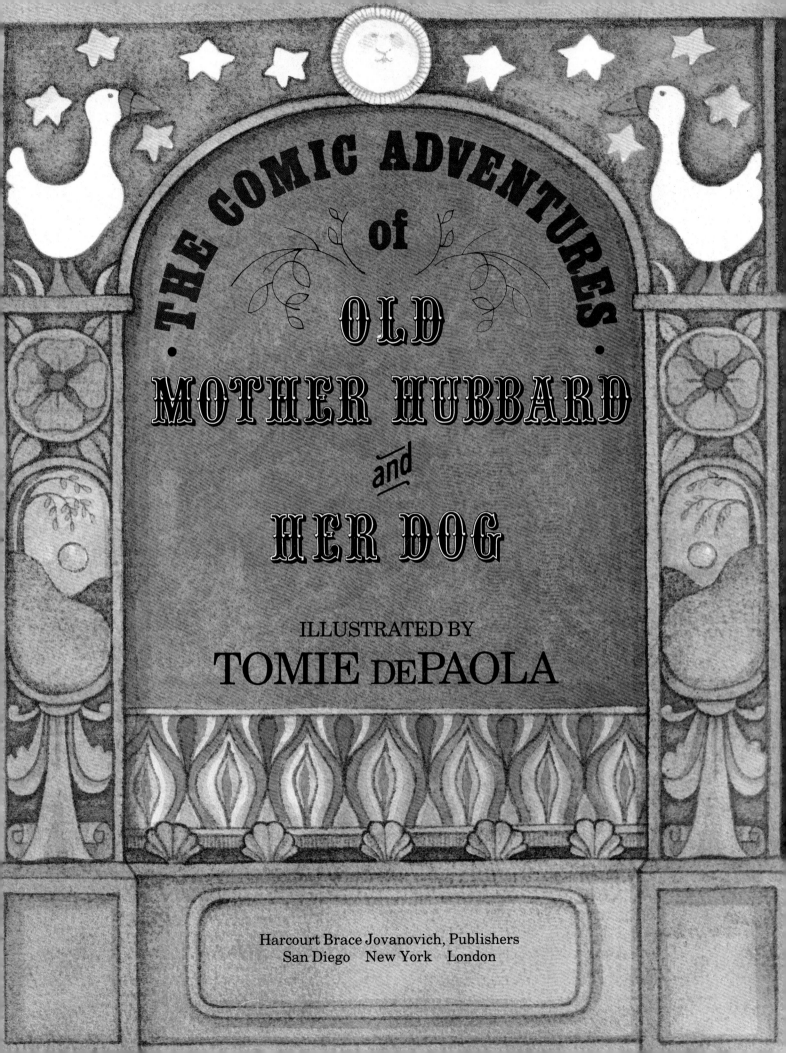

THE COMIC ADVENTURES
of
OLD
MOTHER HUBBARD
and
HER DOG

ILLUSTRATED BY

TOMIE dePAOLA

Harcourt Brace Jovanovich, Publishers
San Diego   New York   London

FOR MARGARET MARY

Printed in Hong Kong

Library of Congress Cataloging in Publication Data
Martin, Sarah Catherine, 1768-1826. The comic
adventures of Old Mother Hubbard and her dog.
SUMMARY: Old Mother Hubbard runs errand after errand
for her remarkable dog.
1. Nursery rhymes, English.   2. Children's poetry,
English.   [1. Nursery rhymes]
I. De Paola, Thomas Anthony.   II. Title.
PR4984.M2804   1981   398′.8   80-19270

ISBN 0-15-219541-6   ISBN 0-15-219542-4 (pbk.)

C D E F   C D E F (pbk.)

Old Mother Hubbard
Went to the cupboard
To fetch her poor dog a bone;
But when she got there
The cupboard was bare,
And so the poor dog had none.

She went to the baker's
To buy him some bread;

But when she came back
The poor dog was dead.

She went to the undertaker's
To buy him a coffin;

But when she came back
The poor dog was laughing.

She took a clean dish
To get him some tripe;

But when she came back
He was smoking a pipe.

She went to the fishmonger's
To buy him some fish;

But when she came back
He was licking the dish.

She went to the tavern
For white wine and red;

But when she came back
The dog stood on his head.

She went to the fruiterer's
To buy him some fruit;

But when she came back
He was playing the flute.

She went to the tailor's
To buy him a coat;

But when she came back
He was riding a goat.

She went to the hatter's
To buy him a hat;

But when she came back
He was feeding the cat.

She went to the barber's
To buy him a wig;

But when she came back
He was dancing a jig.

She went to the cobbler's
To buy him some shoes;

But when she came back
He was reading the news.

She went to the seamstress
To buy him some linen;

But when she came back
The dog was a-spinning.

She went to the hosier's
To buy him some hose;

But when she came back
He was dressed in his clothes.

The dame made a curtsy,
The dog made a bow;

The dame said, "Your servant,"
The dog said, "Bow-wow."

THE END